THREAD OF Love

WITHDRAWN

written by
Kabir Sehgal & Surishtha Sehgal

illustrated by
Zara Gonzalez Hoang

BEACH LANE BOOKS • New York   London   Toronto   Sydney   New Delhi

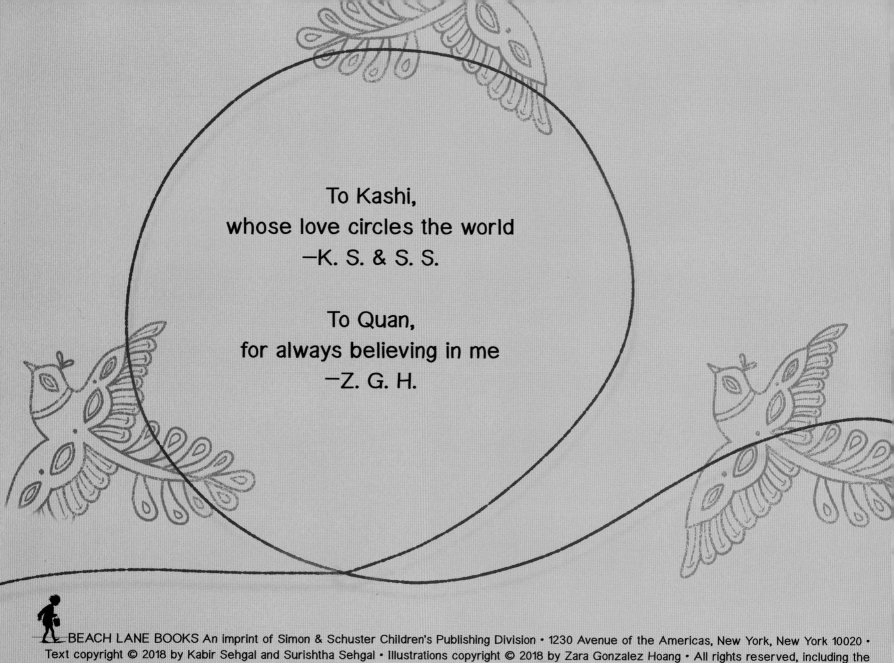

To Kashi,
whose love circles the world
—K. S. & S. S.

To Quan,
for always believing in me
—Z. G. H.

BEACH LANE BOOKS An imprint of Simon & Schuster Children's Publishing Division • 1230 Avenue of the Americas, New York, New York 10020 • Text copyright © 2018 by Kabir Sehgal and Surishtha Sehgal • Illustrations copyright © 2018 by Zara Gonzalez Hoang • All rights reserved, including the right of reproduction in whole or in part in any form. • BEACH LANE BOOKS is a trademark of Simon & Schuster, Inc. • For information about special discounts for bulk purchases, please contact Simon & Schuster Special Sales at 1-866-506-1949 or business@ simonandschuster.com. • The Simon & Schuster Speakers Bureau can bring authors to your live event. For more information or to book an event, contact the Simon & Schuster Speakers Bureau at 1-866-248-3049 or visit our website at www.simonspeakers .com. • Book design by Lauren Rille • The text for this book was set in Write. • The artwork in this book was created digitally in Photoshop with liberal use of the undo button. • Manufactured in China • 0718 SCP • First Edition • 10 9 8 7 6 5 4 3 2 1 Library of Congress Cataloging-in-Publication Data • Names: Sehgal, Kabir, author. | Sehgal, Surishtha, author. | Hoang, Zara Gonzalez, illustrator. • Title: Thread of love / Kabir Sehgal and Surishtha Sehgal ; illustrated by Zara Gonzalez Hoang. • Description: First edition. | New York : Beach Lane Books, [2018] | Summary: Three siblings enjoy the Indian festival of Raksha Bandhan, a celebration of the special relationship between brothers and sisters, in this reinterpretation of the song "Frère Jacques." • Identifiers: LCCN 2017046779 | ISBN 9781534404731 (hardcover : alk. paper) • ISBN 9781534404748 (eBook) • Subjects: LCSH: Children's songs, English—United States—Texts. | CYAC: Festivals—Songs and music. | Brothers and sisters—Songs and music. | India—Songs and music. | Songs. • Classification: LCC PZ8.3.S455 Th 2018 | DDC 782.42 [E]—dc23 LC record available at https://lccn.loc.gov/2017046779

Raksha Bandhan or *rakhi*, which is pronounced "rah-KEY," is an Indian festival in which brothers and sisters celebrate their love and respect for each other. Sisters give brothers a thread bracelet called a *rakhi*, which represents their love. Brothers promise to care for their sisters and give them presents like sweets, jewelry, toys, and clothes.

Are you sleeping,
are you sleeping,

Brother Ji?
Brother Ji?

Morning bells are ringing.
Morning bells are ringing.

DING
DING
DONG

DING
DING
DONG

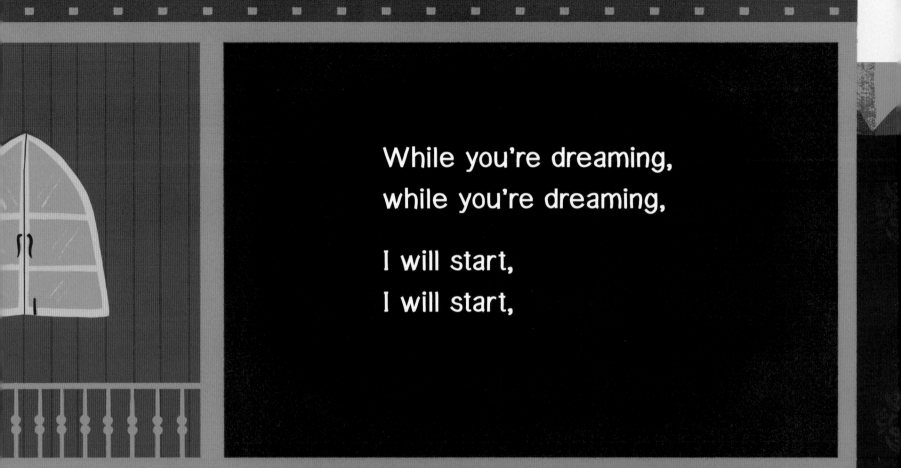

While you're dreaming,
while you're dreaming,

I will start,
I will start,

making you a *rakhi*,
making you a *rakhi*,

thread of love,
thread of love.

weave the threads together, weave the threads together.

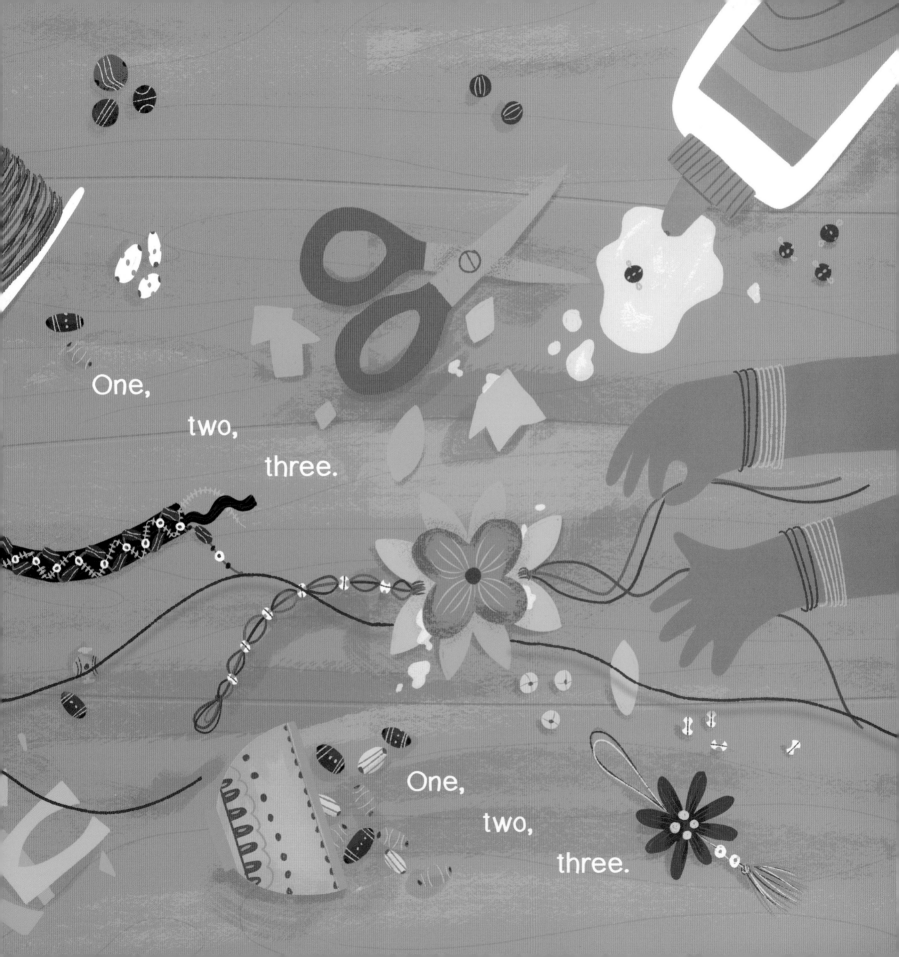

One,

two,

three.

One,

two,

three.

Sparkle, glitter.
Sparkle, glitter.

Sequins glow.
Sequins glow.

Don't forget the tassel!
Don't forget the tassel!

Swish, swish, swish.   Swish, swish, swish.

Here's your *rakhi*.
Here's your *rakhi*.

I will tie.
I will tie.

Hope you keep it always,
hope you keep it always,

thread of love,
thread of love.

Sister Kashi,
Sister Kashi,

meri ban,
meri ban,

Have a tasty chum chum.
Have a tasty chum chum.

Sweet, sweet, treat.
Sweet, sweet, treat.

Brothers, sisters. Brothers, sisters.

Cousins, too.

Cousins, too.

NORTH AMERICA

SOUTH AMERICA

Family, friends,
and neighbors.
Family, friends,
and neighbors,

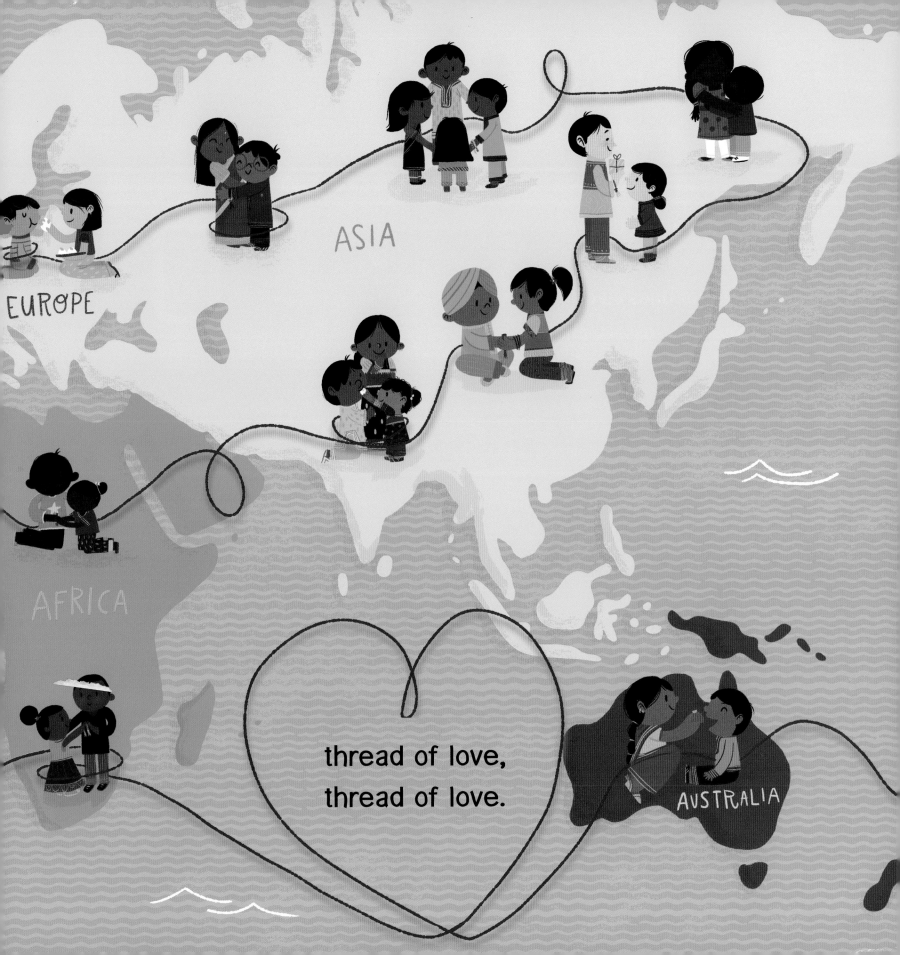

EUROPE

ASIA

AFRICA

thread of love,
thread of love.

AUSTRALIA

DO YOU WANT TO MAKE A RAKHI?

YOU'LL NEED

- Colored embroidery thread
- Scissors
- Craft glue that dries clear
- Beads, sequins, tassels, charms, bells, glitter — whatever decorations you like!

INSTRUCTIONS

1 Pick three or more threads and cut them to about fourteen inches long. Tie them together with a knot on one end, big enough that your decorations won't slip off. (You may need to make more than one knot.)

2 Weave or braid the threads together.

3 Thread the rakhi through the decorations you've picked out, spacing the decorations evenly. Use glue or knots on either side to anchor them.

4 When you reach the end of the rakhi, finish it with another knot, like the one you made in step 1.

5 Add spots of glue and top them with glitter.

6 Let the rakhi dry.

7 Tie the rakhi on a family member or friend—and spread the love!

GLOSSARY

Ji: a sign of respect

Chum chum: a type of Indian sweet

Meri ban: "My sister." An alternate spelling for "*ban*" is "*behan.*"

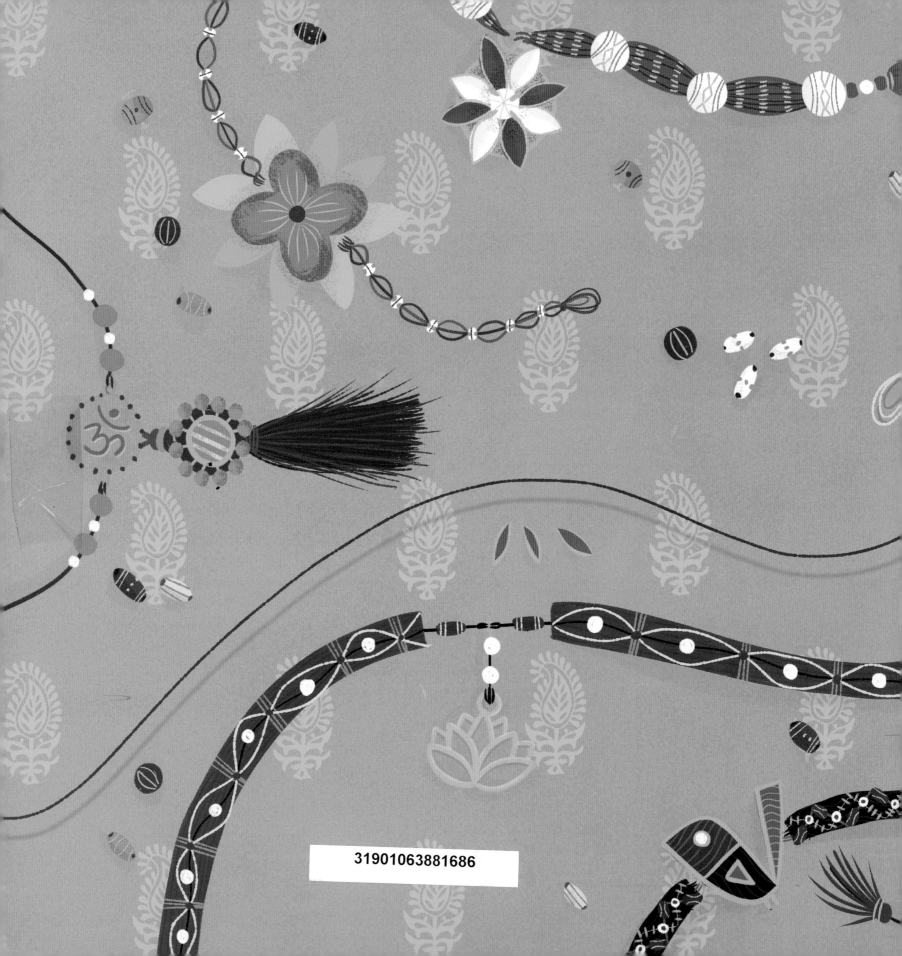